For all Urhammers—
Bette, Nils, Susanne, Peter, and Marianne

Peter and the Troll Baby

by Jan Wahl   •   illustrated by Erik Blegvad

A GOLDEN BOOK • NEW YORK
Western Publishing Company, Inc., Racine, Wisconsin 53404

Peter and his family were going on a trip.
Ashore, Grandma waved to Peter, baby Susanna, and Mother and Father. Falun the dog was tied up below deck.

"I love Susanna," said Peter. "But why can't she stay home with Grandma? She'll spoil our vacation," he grumbled. "She's too *little.*"

"Why, Peter, see how she smiles at you," said Mother. Susanna held his thumb tightly.

"Don't let the trolls take her!" called Grandma.

Slowly *The Star* pulled out.
The pier faded away and the ship
slid down the deep fjords between
the steep flinty mountains.

In the pale night the ship seemed to shimmer.
Then, at sunrise, the mountains hovered
mysterious gray and frosted pink.
The trip north was over.

The family stayed in a yellow wood cottage.
The first morning as breakfast cooked, Peter
cried, "Hey! Somebody looked in our window!"
But Mother found only broken flowers.
"It was the cow, Son," she said, laughing.
Falun barked at odd footprints near the bushes.

Later, while Mother rode the horse Sigurd,
Peter had to mind Susanna. "Ugh," he snorted.
He lay on the grass beside his sister
and watched Father paint.
"Are there *really* trolls around here?" Peter asked.
"I think I just saw one scooting away."
Father shook his head. "That's only a story, Son.
It's said they're made of twigs and moss—
they have long tails and lumpy toes."
Peter sighed. "I'm tired of watching Susanna.
I wish a big troll *would* snatch her!"
"Be glad we have her," Father said.

In the deep of night in the dark room
he shared with Susanna, Peter heard something.
He thought he saw bright red eyes
blinking at him.
    He hid under his blanket,
slowly counting to ninety-nine.
Falun whimpered.
    Shuffle…shuffle…
Soon all grew silent.

At daybreak the baby bawled,
screeched, kicked.
   Peter got up to comfort her.
   "THAT'S NOT MY SISTER!" he gasped—
and ran to fetch his parents.

Side by side they stood and gazed
at the red-faced thing.

Father said, "She's probably teething."

Mother said, "Of course it's Susanna.
She has a tummy ache."

She picked her up. "She *is* heavy."

"This is my fault," mumbled Peter.
"I never should have wished it. Trolls
can't help stealing, can they?"

"They are famous for it," said Father.

All that day the troll baby bellowed.
Peter scrambled onto Sigurd.
"Where are you going?" shouted Mother.
"To save my true sister! Come, Falun!"

And off Peter flew on Sigurd, galloping
away to the forest.

After a time the sun began to sink.
The shadows lay long.
Owls hooted. Toads croaked.
Peter stopped once, to pick some berries.

At last they came to a clear stream.
On the other side a gray troll squatted, crayfishing.
   Slow-witted trolls trudged back and forth,
pulling stolen cows, sheep, and goats.
   Peter tied Sigurd to a stump.
 "Quiet, Falun. Stay!"
   He crawled near and hid by a log.
   On the far bank, a troll mother sat
with her hairy tail lolling in the water.
She sang, "*Lullay, lullay. Hush, hush.*"
In her huge hands she held a pale baby.
Susanna!
   "How will I ever get her away?" groaned Peter.

Suddenly Troll Mother tossed Susanna
high up in the air like a rag doll!
With a gap-toothed grin another troll
caught her and threw her back.
Susanna laughed gaily.

Although it was summer, each cottage
wore thick snow on the roof.

Cooing, Troll Mother took Susanna
into one of the houses.

Some of the trolls shuffled off to bed. Others slept outside, guarding livestock and chests of gold.

Gingerly Peter crossed the stream and grabbed a fat, thorny stick.

Quietly he crept forward.
As soon as Troll Mother was snoring,
Peter pushed her window ajar.
Susanna lay sleeping in a trough
of soft straw.
Peter hooked a long thorn
into her gown, lifting her up and out
through the window. She was still asleep.

Oh! He stepped on a tail!
At once the trolls awoke with a growl.
Their giant eyes flashed lightning.
Slowly the awful trolls began to stir
as Peter skipped back across the stream
on the small, wet stones.

"CATCH HIM!" came a roar like thunder.
"It is the end of us," thought Peter,
jumping onto Sigurd. "*Hurry*, Falun!"
It did no good to yell.
The angry trolls hopped behind Sigurd,
who galloped for dear life now.

"*Faster*, Sigurd!"
Pine needles scratched. The ground shook.
White and huge, the moon rose ahead.
Susanna was small, and she felt so warm
in Peter's arms.
The trolls rumbled closer!

As if by magic, Peter reached home first.
The door was unlocked. Father and Mother
had waited up, for they could not
sleep with Peter away.
   "Look!" Peter yelled.
"I've got my *true* sister!"

Quickly he set the red-faced troll baby
out on the steps. It was so surprised
it forgot to scream.

Grunting and puffing, the trolls thumped up.
"HERE SHE IS!" they bawled.

Troll Mother grabbed her own child, thinking
she had Susanna, and away the trolls hopped
in triumph.

At last Peter climbed into his bed.
Father smiled. "Son, you are brave."
"How *could* I make such a mistake?"
asked Mother. "Of course, this
is Susanna."
Each hugged Susanna in turn.
Falun danced.

But always afterward—whenever his sister lay
howling, kicking, tomato-faced—
Peter wondered
if she were Susanna or . . .

the troll baby?